Oh Lord... Paint My Room

Gladys Evans Peoples, PhD

Copyright © 2020 by Gladys Evans Peoples, PhD
Oh Lord...Paint My Room
gladyspeoples@yahoo.com

All rights reserved. In accordance with the U.S. Copyright Act of 1976, the scanning, uploading, and electronic sharing of any part of this book without the permission of the publisher is unlawful piracy and theft of the author's intellectual property. If you would like to use material from the book, prior written permission must be obtained by contacting the publisher at info@entegritypublishing.com.

Thank you for your support of the author's rights.

The views expressed in this work are solely those of the author and do not necessarily reflect the views of the publisher, and the publisher hereby disclaims any responsibility for them.

Entegrity Choice Publishing
PO Box 453
Powder Springs, GA 30127
info@entegritypublishing.com
www.entegritypublishing.com
770.727.6517

Printed in the United States of America

Library of Congress Cataloging-in-Publication Data
ISBN 978-1-7351739-1-7
Library of Congress Control Number: 2020912669

Dedication

This book is dedicated to my children: Pancakes, Cupcakes, No Cakes, and Pound Cake. It was through our turbulent time, Saturday paint samples, and weekend room makeovers that God outlined the details for this book. He has continuously used each of you to develop me and for that, I am grateful. Thank you for understanding the quiet time required to pen this work. It is my sincerest prayer that you will seek God daily with total submission and genuine longing to have a pure heart before Him. Always remember, man looks at the outward appearance, but God looks at the heart. (1 Samuel 16:7)

This book is also dedicated to every person who yearns to have a clean heart that is acceptable to God. I pray that the simple words, painting parallels, and step-by-step techniques provided in this book will supply you clarity and understanding for gaining and keeping a clean heart before God.

Acknowledgements

With genuine reverence, beyond adequate expressions, I thank my Abba Father for selecting me to pen His words.

I offer loving thanks to my favorite son, Titus, for the sketched details presented on the book cover.

Contents

Dedication iii
Acknowledgements v
Introduction ix

Chapter 1
    Heart Cost 19
    Step 1: Making the Decision .29

Chapter 2
    Heart Colors 31
    Step 2: Accepting Your Hue 38

Chapter 3
    Heart Cleanse 41
    Step 3: Discarding the Elephants 45

Chapter 4
    Heart Attack 47
    Step 4: Taking a Deep Dive 53

Chapter 5
    Heart Stent 55
    Step 5: Receiving the Strokes .61

Chapter 6
    Heart Recovery 63
    Step 6: Coming Together Again 66

Chapter 7
    Heart Maintenance 69
    Step 7: Retaining Your Health 73

Chapter 8
    Summary 75
    Summary 78

Introduction
The Question

Have you ever walked into your bedroom and silently screamed: *these walls absolutely must be painted!?* The color is bland, uninspiring, and a bit depressing. It doesn't enhance the flooring or even begin to provide a welcoming, serene atmosphere to relax. And to top it off, close inspection divulges that the walls not only have a multitude of imperfections, but they are just dirty.

Or perhaps you often close your child's bedroom door because even though you've cleaned the room, it still looks unkempt. Every leap on the transformed trampoline bed left the surrounding walls scantily decorated with black marks and dents. Throughout the room—from the crown molding to the baseboards—random wall dimples are visible from the multitude of balls hurled by the self-proclaimed professional 3rd grade racquetball player.

Even more, the walls reveal evidence of the abuse endured from the pink pig toy box that is regularly emptied to locate that one must-have toy that is noiselessly resting behind the chest. The truth is, the walls in any child's room and almost all regularly occupied areas become worn with use and unappealing as time passes.

The Home Makeover

You might wonder what prompted me to pay such close attention to my walls. Truthfully, after my divorce was legally finalized, I began to declutter, rearrange, and paint each room in my house. It was an effort to revitalize and start living anew with an updated and fresh environment. It was a concentrated endeavor to transform the living space in my home. It's common that it takes a major life change to alert us to what has been a permanent fixture right in front of us. The COVID-19 pandemic is a prime example. For many families in forced quarantine, there has been an in-depth awakening—a renewed awareness of each individual's value and a revitalized importance of respecting and supporting the family unit. Unfortunately, on the other hand, some couples come to realize that they have no connection at all, beyond the shared bills and marriage title. Although most of the confined families have occupied the same space for years, like my walls, they failed to detect what was present all along.

Nonetheless, I began my home transformation by hiring a semi-professional painter to cover my dirty, flat, eggshell walls (you know, the bland color every apartment and non-custom home is painted) with a calm, cool-toned, yet warm paint that offered an immediate shift in the atmosphere: Sherwin-Williams semi-gloss *Tony Taupe*.

After all this time, I find it utterly amazing that I still recall the color as if I selected it yesterday. I did not study the assortment or even pause when making the choice. I spotted the hue from the color palette and selected it almost immediately. I sensed it would offer an astounding alteration in not only the décor, but my mood. I believe this color has been etched in my mind as a symbolic representation that marked the genesis of a major life shift.

Introduction

As I penned these words, I felt it necessary to research the color choice. Hence, it is noteworthy to mention that the name *Tony* means praiseworthy or of inestimable worth; while the word *Taupe* originates from a French noun meaning mole. The color is a mixture of browns and greys and said to be warm, timeless, practical, modest, organic, and authentic.

Color psychologists claim that individuals who choose taupe are said to be dependable, classic, humble, and down-to-earth. Additionally, while the taupe selectors tend to avoid excess attention, they are empathetic toward others, easy for others to connect to, conservative, and cautious. Astonishingly, I did praise God for the peace and refreshed atmosphere the color offered, and the stated attributes align with my personality and character in almost all ways! I challenge you to review the selected colors in your home. How do they confirm or conflict with your personality and core values? More importantly, what color and heart changes do you need to make to mark the beginning of positive modifications in your life?

Be that as it may, with the entrance, den, and stairwell painted, the remainder of the house looked atrocious and the attempted makeover was blatantly incomplete. The remaining toddler fingerprints, scuffed walls, and stained spots were highlighted beyond tolerance, so I began the quest to paint the remainder of the house room by room. After watching my semi-professional painter paint such large areas with nine feet high ceilings, I concluded I could surely transform the other, much smaller rooms.

The Weekends

For several months, I had a Saturday routine. My four children and I would make a mid-day trip to Lowes and/or Walmart to muddle through massive color palettes and select samples of

Oh Lord...Paint My Room

various hues. Each of my children would select her/his favorite color, often changing weekly, for the new room. I would purchase supplies, take the kids to lunch, usually at Chick-Fil-A, and then head home and unload the materials in the garage. The following Friday, I would drop my babies off at their father's residence at precisely 5 pm, pick up fast food, and rush home to begin my 48-hour room makeover before they returned.

At the time, I didn't realize the therapeutic implications. As I discarded old, worn, seldom-used items in preparation for a more tidy, inviting, and efficient room, God was exposing and disposing my unnecessary attitudes and negative character traits and repairing my broken heart as the initial groundwork for the new me. This makes me wonder if there are antiquated, worn out, and unused items in your home and/or *heart* that need discarding? This would be a good time to examine your home and your heart with reflection and pray for revelatory insight.

The Revelation

My revelation came during the third watch of the night. It was approximately 1 am on a fall Saturday morning. I had just finished painting the first coat of *Favorite Jeans* semi-glossy paint on the walls of my daughters' shared space. Their master bedroom-sized room had taken hours to prep. After I gathered all the Barbies, stuffed animals, and toys scattered throughout the room, I repaired dents, light sanded, and spot primed. I removed switch and electrical covers and used painter's tape to edge the ceiling and baseboards. Everything had been pushed to the center of the massive space and I maneuvered all my supplies and painted around the heap with ease. I decided to sit on their baby blue stool to rest and survey my work. As soon as I sat down, the Holy Spirit began to show me step by step how my own heart was like this room. The four chambers of my heart needed a makeover, not just a dose of Jesus, but removal of the waste, scraping of the corners, patching of the holes, buffing of the walls, and primer to seal the very presence of God. The parallel was amazingly specific, clear, and sure.

A Heart for All Seasons

It was from this bedroom-makeover experience that this book was formed. While this book provides the methodology used to prepare and properly paint a room, this process is not the intended main focus. The instructions and suggestions discussed for painting a room are detailed to assist you with understanding the primary emphasis, God's heart renewal process. Thus, this book will provide you with a clear understanding of the parallels between painting a room and God's cleaning, patching, sealing, and rejuvenating of the human heart.

If you secretly know the rooms of your heart have become dull, uninviting, or even darkened by the stains of your sin or the destructive impact of others, this book is for you. If you're dressed up on the outside and worried you may end up in hell, this book is for you. If you are trapped in a routine, lack enthusiasm for the things of God, or can't remember the last time you felt genuine in your relationship with God, this book is a must read for you.

Oh Lord…Paint My Room will usher you through the deep recesses of your heart to receive a renewed, revitalized, and loving heart that is submitted and committed to God. Your reconstruction will fill your heart with joy and peace that will allow you to optimistically experience summer's rays, fall's invigorating wind, the purity of winter's first snowfall, and spring's refreshing rain. In fact, He consistently and lovingly extends an open invitation to participate in His facelift process that mends and beautifies less-than-pure hearts.

The overarching purpose of this book is to create a longing for God to paint the chambers of your heart and produce an acceptance for each segment of the process to complete His work.

> *"Being confident of this, that He who began a good work in you will carry it on to completion until the day of Christ Jesus." Philippians 1:6*

God promises to complete His work in us, grow us in grace, and never give up on us. It doesn't matter how moldy the walls have become beneath the surface or even if some of your walls are missing, God can repair the rooms of your heart and paint them to perfection. He will not force Himself into your heart, but He is readily available if you want His beautification.

A Purified Heart

Oh Lord…Paint My Room is an inspired revelation that provides a simplistic glimpse into the multilayered intricacies of the behaviors and beliefs that flow from the human heart and the methods by which they can be cleaned, healed, sealed, and transformed by God. This book compares the procedures used to prepare and paint a room to the process God uses to transform and reestablish the broken, contrite, or confused hearts of His children.

Much like the build-up of dirt, life circumstances can influence us to acquire negative attitudes, defensive mechanisms, and heart calluses—and much like the required methods used to adequately prepare and paint a room, the build-up must be removed by God for optimized use of our lives. This book will teach you how to obtain a clean heart free of debris, regretful behaviors, and faulty thinking.

Introduction

*"Create in me a clean heart, O God,
and renew a right spirit within me." Psalm 51:10*

In other words, David's request of God was to make his heart pure and his spirit steadfast, faithful, and loyal. For David knew that God examines and selects His servants based on the heart, rather than outward appearance.

*"But the LORD said to Samuel, Do not consider his appearance or his height, for I have rejected him. The LORD does not look at the things people look at. People look at the outward appearance, but the LORD looks at the heart."
I Samuel 16:7*

The request and passionate plea of every believer ought to be for our omnipotent God to purify our hearts.

Clean Heart Benefits

He will decorate your attitudes, beliefs, character, and relationships, making them fresh and brand new from a pure heart, while producing a modernized, classic facelift of your interior and exterior. The Bible is clear that what we say and do comes from the outpouring of what resides in the core of our hearts. Jesus Himself said, *"A good man brings good things out of the good stored up in his heart, and an evil man brings evil things out of the evil stored up in his heart. For the mouth speaks what the heart is full of."* (Luke 6:45) Jesus further explains to His disciples that there is a connection between what people speak and their hearts, *"But the things that come out of a person's mouth come from the heart, and these defile them. For out of the heart come evil thoughts—murder, adultery, sexual immorality, theft, false testimony, slander. These are what defile a person; but eating with unwashed hands does not defile them."* (Matthew 15:18-20) Hence, there is a certain necessity to obtain and maintain a genuine, wholesome heart. Given that everything you do and say comes from your heart, why would you resist God's desire to renovate and paint your heart with His perfect presence?

Moreover, if given permission, God will produce a heart that can give and receive genuine love without continuous guard and doubt of authenticity. He will remove and restore your heart to live your life to the fullest with 1 Corinthians 13:4-7 oozing from your essence.

"Love is patient, love is kind. It does not envy, it does not boast, it is not proud. It does not dishonor others, it is not self-seeking, it is not easily angered, it keeps no record of wrongs. Love does not delight in evil but rejoices with the truth. It always protects, always trusts, always hopes, always perseveres." 1 Corinthians 13:4-7

You must examine your own heart and questions yourself. Are there areas that need to be refurbished, scrapped clean, or repaired? Are you willing to submit to God's process for renovating your heart? If the answers to these questions are yes, *Oh Lord...Paint My Room*, will provide you with a deep dive and a specific step-by-step, how-to map for your heart reconstruction.

The Paint Master

If you have ever painted a room, I mean completed all the tasks required for painting a room, you know that the job is never as simple as it initially seems. Painting a room to produce unblemished, lasting results is an art that requires time, hard work, and determination without compromise on the products or the process. Just the same, while God could and did change Saul's heart and disposition of mind instantaneously *"as Saul turned to leave Samuel, God changed Saul's heart, and all these signs were fulfilled that day."*

Introduction

(I Samuel 10:9), a renovated heart typically involves a process over extended time with complete willingness of the recipient.

If you are a proficient painter, this book will lead you to understand the corresponding spiritual implications of the room painting process at a depth that is clear and detailed. Furthermore, if you have a room with sample colors on the walls, tape around the door frame, one section painted, electrical outlets uncovered, or unfinished in any way; this book will create a yearning in you for a finished room and the completion of God's work in your own heart. You will find yourself excited about anticipated room results and the possibilities of the new you.

If you have never painted a room but would like to try it; this book will help you understand the necessity of following the appropriate steps to produce the desired results in your room and your heart. You will discover that cutting corners or skipping steps will produce the mere appearance of a completed room and refurbished heart, but ultimately you will be forced to start the process over to get lasting results. Finally, if you currently have absolutely no desire to ever paint a room; this book will build your curiosity, stir up a desire for renovated rooms in your life, and cause you to aggressively seek *The Paint Master*.

1
Heart Cost

Step 1: Making the Decision

Decision Makers

Every outcome, whether good or bad, requires some type of input. Before every input, there is a decision to act that originates from a thought. For example, if you have a new vehicle, there was first an idea that you needed or wanted a car, a verdict to buy it, and a negotiation to purchase. Or perhaps you baked a cake; there was a desire for something sweet, followed by a decision to mix the ingredients. And finally, a bake of the elements to produce the outcome: cake.

Fundamentally regardless of the ending, the genesis is an idea or knowing, followed by a preference, and finally an input that results in a conclusion. This developmental procedure is the first necessary step for not only painting a room, but also renovation of your heart. You need a made-up mind followed by actions to pursue and suitable contributions if you want a transformed room or clean heart.

The original recognition that the rooms were imperfect and needed a color makeover led to my declaration that painting the rooms was a necessity. Correspondingly, you may feel unsettled, disgusted by your own actions or sense you are on the road to nowhere with little hope of survival. With this awareness in mind, it is hoped that you have been prompted to recognize that modifications of your actions and heart are essential to cancel the impending toxic outcome just on the horizon. That is, to miss your God-prescribed destiny and spend your life realizing there is more, but you can never reach it.

Is the Result Worth It?

Regardless of the decisions made, whether to freshen the walls in your home or the chambers of your heart, all rulings should carefully consider the associated time, labor, and cost required for completion. Even more, each of these individual factors have to be deemed worthwhile for the desired outcome before beginning the project. Thus, the result must be worth the required input. Jesus models this concept by teaching us to also consider all aspects, including details and sacrifices before making our commitment to Him. Luke 14:28-30 emphasizes counting the cost of discipleship and weighing the price of building completion.

> *"Suppose one of you wants to build a tower. Won't you first sit down and estimate the cost to see if you have enough money to complete it? For if you lay the foundation and are not able to finish it, everyone who sees it will ridicule you saying, This person began to build and wasn't able to finish."*
> *Luke 14:28-30*

All too often, we have random ideas that influence us to make decisions or cause us to change a course of action, without considering the accompanying tangible or emotional expense. We see with our eyes, desire, and move forward on a whim to an anticipated end that may or may not be what we expect.

Doesn't this sound amazingly similar to the account of Eve and the fall of man recorded in Genesis? *"When the woman saw that the fruit of the tree was good for food and pleasing to the eye, and also desirable for gaining wisdom, she took some and ate it. She also gave some to her husband, who was with her, and he ate it."* (Genesis 3:6)

Perhaps we shouldn't be so quick to judge her or others when we often follow suit with our own decision-making patterns. We make frivolous purchases without regard of the budget or the need to save, exchange relationships without growth-time consideration, and participate in blatantly sinful activities without admission of our ever-present God. Simply stated, we habitually fail to carefully reflect on all facets of our ideas or calculate the cost of our decisions before we act.

Honest Assessment

While choosing whether or not to paint a room is a rather menial choice, your decision to have your heart transformed is life altering and should involve a meticulous approach. After all, this revolution will not only create a revitalized heart, but also a renewed mind and changed thinking patterns. The results will create an attitude that embraces the statement, "The things I used to do, I don't do any more."

In addition, although one could hire someone to do the painting and obtain spectacular results with little effort, the heart transplant is a personal choice, a surrendering of your desires that will most assuredly cost you something, or some things that far exceed the value of money. Every individual must decide if they are willing to allow God to renovate the very core of her being. Judicious consideration and serious questions with honest responses should be taken into account for this verdict.

Is rebuilding worth the asking price? Does the tradeoff value exceed the relinquishing of everything, including your unaligned plans and goals and a few relationships? Does having a pure heart before God outweigh your desires to do what you please, when you please and with whom you please? Is the final output worth the cost of your input?

I recognize these are momentous, challenging questions that require serious reflection, abandonment of oneself, and certainly God's grace to respond with a firm yes. I also know, however, that failure to adequately self-assess will likely lead to collapse on your journey to your clean heart. Be that as it may, you undoubtedly need to pause, pray, and peruse your true heart's desire.

Without compromise, to walk in the center of God's will in your predetermined purpose with a clean heart, you are required to want God more than anything! Exclusively, you need Him to be first, the focus of your life and the GPS for your journey. This means surrendering your longings and allowing God to fill you with what to desire, so you can be launched into your destiny. The Bible reminds us to *"Delight thyself also in the LORD: and he shall give thee the desires of thine heart."* (Psalm 37:4 KJV) This scripture indicates if you truly want a pure heart, you must confess your sins and relinquish everything to God for His molding and shaping. With consistent devotion to God, He will fill your heart with that which you need to complete the purpose for which you were born. Additionally, just as Jeremiah was formed, known by God before he was born, and set apart to be a prophet to the nations (Jeremiah 1:5), you too were born for a specific purpose and destiny.

> *"For those God foreknew he also predestined to be conformed to the image of his Son, that he might be the firstborn among many brothers and sisters. And those he predestined, he also called; those he called, he also justified; those he justified, he also glorified. What, then, shall we*

say in response to these things? If God is for us, who can be against us?" Romans 8:29-31

The Bible is clear that each and every one of us, *including you,* have a divine purpose on the earth and God's master plan cannot be thwarted when His will and directions are received. *"I will cry to God Most High, Who accomplishes all things on my behalf for He completes my purpose in His plan."* (Psalm 57:2 AMP)

As a result of the weightiness and consequences of this decision, you can't announce that you want to be changed, cleaned, or shaped from a mere momentary idea. This decision should be a selection, declaration, and commitment that's birthed from research of God's word, deep deliberation, and surrender to become a new, improved, and best you.

Don't Quit

Unfortunately, many people (and perhaps you, too) have stopped mid-way on the journey, cut corners, or simply did not start, concluding it is too difficult, will take too long, or your heart is too dark. Others reject God's offer and hang their excuse on "I'm not ready yet," "This is just the way I am," "This is too hard," or "God would never want to use me, I've done too much." Please know if these have been your excuses, defenses, or fears, you can exhale with confidence because God wants to dwell within you just as much as He resides in those you have regarded as worthy to receive His love.

God's Work

There is no option to alter some behaviors on your own. You can't merely stop cursing, smoking, fornicating, etc., and go to church to renovate you own heart. While modifying the behaviors you know are displeasing to God is important, your adjustments will not disinfect your heart. God's purification involves a much deeper cleanse than the altering of apparent unaligned God-required actions.

Your efforts and His cleansing are like the difference between getting your teeth cleaned under normal bi-yearly circumstances by the dental hygienist verses the dentist performing periodontal scaling to eliminate the hidden tartar buildup that has silently led to infection in the gums. While hygienists primarily clean teeth and check patients for oral diseases, more serious problems such as tarter cleansing is performed by the licensed dentist. Often unbeknownst to the hygienists, the dentist understands without proper treatment, pockets will form at the gum line and create bone decay and eventual tooth loss.

Equally, God's deep-rooted cleanse washes away that which most others cannot see and ofttimes that of which even you are unaware. Thus, the hygienist (you) performs surface work, while the dentist (God) eradicates the root causes, stops death, and creates as healthy mouth. Our hearts contain dispositions and calluses comparable to the tartar buildup that, without God's removal, will eventually lead to corruption and loss of our purposed life. Simply stated, God alone renovates the heart with complete and total surrender as payment for the revolutionary makeover. While you can transmute a room, you truly do not have the capacity to transform your own heart. Heart work is God's work.

Further, because your heart is renovated by God alone, only He knows what needs to be removed and what is required to construct your heart from the foundation upward. You can only estimate the time, behavioral adjustments, and altered thinking patterns essential for the transformation.

Heart Condition/Repair Time

Like the expense incurred for painting a room, the renovated heart payment is more than the monetary commitment for paint. To paint a room, there must be consideration of the physical labor, as well as the time required to complete the task based on the size and condition of the room. What type of room is it? Are there fixed items on the walls? Are there odd angles? Are the walls damaged with visible dents, scrapes, or holes? Are you painting the entire room or only an accent wall? The answers to these questions directly impact the total overhead in supplies, time, and labor.

Comparatively, the condition of your heart influences the size and scope of the renovation. For example, if you have lived a life in direct opposition to God with little reverence of Him; a total makeover may be mandatory with wall demolitions. That is, creating a heart reflective of God's love will likely dictate a shift in your values, beliefs, and lifestyle. Perhaps you self-sabotage, over-indulge, or live to uphold your ungodly family cultures and deem God as low on your list of priorities.

On the other hand, you may have been reared in the church and walked in obedience with strong beliefs in God, but now find yourself distant and disconnected. You may currently be an active participant in your local church, serve as an usher, deacon, or minister, and yet feel routine and robot-like without attachment to the Lord Jesus Christ. It is important to examine the condition of your heart closely just as one does when preparing to paint a room. Do you have mold silently destroying your interior walls (and heart) and although you've painted and covered the area before, close evaluation reveals the black spots and a stench remains.

Your own answers to the posed question will give you an idea of the repair needed in your heart. There are countless unique scenarios, past and present, that impact the condition of the heart and the materials and period of time needed to repair it. Being receptive to God's timing is key, as your refusal to respond to His requests and commands will only delay your finish. Your renewal process will be established by God. Rest assured, however, that regardless of your heart state, God is willing and certainly capable of completing the task expertly for the new you.

Authorization

As you count the cost, it is also important to accept that like any interior designer, God will not begin work without your authorization. What does this mean? How do you solicit God's service? Simply thank God for His willingness to cleanse you, tell Him your heart is open to receive and be available for His process. It is stating and adopting His will, while abandoning your own. It is declaring that He knows what's best for you. Although He can and has likely revealed regions of your heart that need an upgrade and zones that need to be demolished and rebuilt, it is imperative to understand that He will not begin construction without your permission.

Trust God's Design

God is the master interior designer and acts similar to most others in creativity and performance. When crafting the brief, designers begin by listening to the homeowner's visions and requests for the room makeover. However, more often than not, nearly all interior engineers have ideals, design details, and finished products that differ from the owner's initial desires. Because the designer has been trained and is experienced with combining patterns, colors, and fabrics far beyond the homeowner, the process and final product usually presents discrepancies from the homeowner's initial vision.

Remarkably though, the end result almost always exceeds

the owner's expectations because the owner has limited understanding of how it all fits together. The interior designer operates and creates with the end in mind, a completed room as the target. The interior designer understands that before the renovation project is complete, the room often looks and feels disastrous without hope of goal attainment. However, they are not concerned because they hold the plans and process for the completed project.

Parallel to the interior designer's room makeover, God, the omniscient room artist, knows our end from the beginning and manipulates and allows our circumstances to set us up with a heart that can be used for His glory.

"I make known the end from the beginning, from ancient times, what is still to come. I say, My purpose will stand, and I will do all that I please." Isaiah 46:10

He knows which materials, people, and experiences to use, as well as when and how to utilize or discard them. It is vital to note that analogous to the room redecoration, during the process, your life and heart may look and feel like a tornado swept through and destroyed everything in place making your life worse.

Nothing is in order as it was before, the space is unsettling—every now and again fear creeps in with regret that the changes were authorized. Moreover, there doesn't seem to be an end in sight and visions of the finished, fresh new space in your heart are faint, at best. Often the questions and statements become, "Why did I allow this? What was I thinking? I can't endure this. This is too chaotic and unsettling for me. I can't find anything. I don't understand what is happening. I just want this to be over."

You absolutely must resist the urge to quit, to fire your interior designer (God) and to put things back in their comfortable stagnant, routine, dull place. Instead, you have to stay focused on the finished product, the improved heart, the fresh and upgraded you. In essence, you must *trust* The Designer to finish His work in your heart. The cost will be worth the finished product.

Meditate on the Word of God

Heart Cost

Step 1: Making the Decision

- Do I <u>*want*</u> a heart renovation?
- Do I <u>*need*</u> a heart renovation?
- Am I willing to surrender my will to receive the upgrade?
- Does the cost outweigh the reward?
- Do I trust God for completion of the project?

If you answered yes to any of the questions above, begin your heart makeover by saying this simple, yet life-changing prayer:

Father,

Thank you for your willingness to cleanse and make me new. I don't understand all the details of your process, the materials you will use to change me, or the final condition of my heart, but I know you want what's best for me. I understand my heart and behavior has to change. I surrender my will to yours and give you permission to renovate my heart. I trust you and know your way is better than mine, in the name of Jesus, amen.

Meditate on the Word of God
Heart Cost

"Yet you, LORD, are our Father. We are the clay; you are the potter; we are all the work of your hand." Isaiah 64:8

"For whoever wants to save their life will lose it, but whoever loses their life for me and for the gospel will save it." Mark 8:35

"And without faith it is impossible to please God, because anyone who comes to him must believe that he exists and that he rewards those who earnestly seek him." Hebrews 11:6

Please take a few moments to quiet yourself and listen. The Lord wants to commune with you. ♡

What is the Holy Spirit saying to you? What was highlighted in this chapter? What words resonated with you? What are your instructions? What do you need to do next?

_____
_____
_____
_____
_____
_____
_____
_____
_____
_____

2
Heart Colors

Step 2: Accepting Your Hue

Paint Finish

Once you have committed to painting the room, your next step is to carefully select your paint finish and color. To obtain the desired outcome, the selection should include consideration of the type of paint finish, including the appearance it produces on the wall and its ability to mask wall imperfections.

For example, flat and textured paints, often used in rental properties, camouflage physical deficiencies, while gloss and semi-gloss paint finishes provide wall sheen, but highlight flaws. If the room has high traffic and requires regular maintenance, gloss and semi-gloss paints are the best choice because they are durable and clean easily.

In contrast, eggshell, flat, and matte paints have low scrub-ability and durability and, therefore, should be used only in low-movement areas to maintain a like-new presence. Satin paint finish hovers in the middle and is recommended for bathrooms, laundry rooms, and children's playrooms. With the information presented, it is undeniably evident that the paint finish selected matters for the type of room you are painting.

Color Impact

The psychological impact of the chosen color and its coordination with the shades in the surrounding environments is also necessary to study before your paint purchase. For instance, color consultants insist that red kitchens stimulate conversation, but also promote hunger; while yellow covered rooms communicate happiness and joy. Light blue and green paints are believed to produce a calm and relaxing atmosphere. Hence, the color choice has the potential to strongly influence the mood in the room and proceeding actions. Additionally, if all the walls in your home are hunter green, painting the family room papaya orange will likely create an unforgiving clash with the adjacent areas.

To create a flow throughout your home, you will need to select colors that complement one another or are a variation of the same hue to provide a seamless progression and harmonious ambience.

Operations in the room and setting should also be taken into account when selecting the paint color. Do you want the room to appear larger, brighter, blend with the external natural environment or provide blanket-like tranquility? Is the space used for exercise, prayer, laundering, relaxation, or family gatherings?

In essence, before selecting a paint color for your walls, reflect on the type of room, usage, and atmosphere you hope to gain from the makeover. The color selected will undoubtedly influence the environmental feel, impact utilization of the room, and effect the surrounding areas; therefore, it should not be selected on an impulse or in isolation, but after thorough research.

Color Caution

Adjacent to selecting your paint color with caution, you must carefully weigh the impact of your heart makeover on your current lifestyle and the receptiveness of others in your circle. What do you plan to change and gain from your heart transplant? What will be different about you? What's in your heart and how do you plan to utilize your upgrade in relation to your acquaintances? These are likely difficult questions to answer at this point because you have yet to witness the final product. However, it is important to ponder the fact that you will not be the same and with these alterations, every acquaintance may not accept or compliment the new you. You lack knowledge of everything that is in your heart or what is going to change, but you can be confident that God will reveal, if you are open to receive, and provide peace as He ushers you through your transformation.

Color Complexity

Just as there are several types of paint finishes and countless color hues, the unique personalities and heart ailments of women are too numerous and complex to adequately identify. I must warn you that although all physical human hearts are colonial brick in color, the color manifested from the heart in the form of behaviors, dispositions, values, and beliefs presents itself through a multitude of hues.

Even more, the color reflected from the human heart is not limited to an independent single shade, but very often a complicated combination. In other words, what we witness and experience from others, while varied in impact and substance, as well as in pleasantries, kindness, and evil, is indicative of the true heart color.

The color state of the heart is shaped by family cultures, positive and negative experiences, foundational beliefs, and multilayered situations woven throughout life's journey. Typically, the heart is molded over time, but just one traumatic event (or a series of traumatic events) can create such an impact that the heart condition is rapidly shifted from its original state to unbalanced and chaotic, much like the vicious aftereffects of a tsunami.

Albeit complex and difficult to pinpoint, I maintain as Jesus taught, that what comes out of a person's mouth and her actions indicate what is housed in her heart (Matthew 15:18; Luke 6:45). This leads us to the challenging section of this chapter. You must determine the color of your heart. Should God commit to your present heart's color and simply refresh the walls with the same shade or is it necessary for Him to select a completely different color to update your heart?

Color Revealed

Regardless of your heart condition or how it was shaped, there are fundamental questions you can ask yourself to assist you with understanding your heart's hue and accepting God's cleansing process. To that end, what does a self-examination of your daily actions and beliefs reveal about your heart? What characteristics do you display that provide evidence about the reality of your heart? Only a deep investigation, honest feedback from trusted confidents, and revelation from the Holy Spirit can deliver the truth regarding your heart.

Once you obtain this information, you will be better able to ascertain God's process. For example, if it is revealed that your heart is unforgiving, it will be easier to understand if God selects to unearth situations and people who hurt you in the past to grow you with acknowledgement and forgiveness. Or perhaps you find that you struggle with pride; God may arrange what you consider lowly or "beneath you" activities and situations to humble you. Simply stated, with identification of your heart's essence, God's techniques are easier to accept.

Without understanding your heart's baggage (color), it will

appear that God is wreaking havoc and punishing you for the sin in your heart, rather than disposing of it. Devoid of heart knowledge, this upheaval will likely cause regret of your submission and influence you to abandon your quest for a new life. I encourage you to embrace the process, endure the revelation, and accept the cleansing. God is disclosing that which is impure in your heart in preparation to remove it and upgrade you. The prophet Isaiah explains this very process for the children of Israel: *"I will turn my hand against you; I will thoroughly purge away your dross and remove all your impurities. I will restore your leaders as in days of old, your rulers as at the beginning. Afterward you will be called the City of Righteousness, the Faithful City."* (Isaiah 1:25-26)

True Color

With recognition of the necessity to examine your heart and receptivity of God's revelation, is your paint color (i.e., personality, character, values, etc.) bright and shiny or dull and boring? Are you the life of the party or do you have improvement comments for everyone, about everything to cover your secret angst and fear that someone will discover your insecurities? Are you critical of others' choices with hidden pride? Do you lived an untamed lifestyle with little to no regard for others because you were hurt deeply as a child and do not trust anyone? Do you want to be able to trust others, including God? Do your confidants regularly tell you that you are selfish, but you want to be more giving? Do you have an "it's-all-about-me" mentality?

These questions require honesty that only you can answer. Failure to acknowledge your true heart condition with an authentic evaluation will result in delayed cleansing. That which you will not acknowledge cannot be changed. What is your true color?

Paint Finish

To further study your heart, it is helpful to review your exterior as related to textured, flat, and matte paint finishes. If you are texture-like in behavior, others are apt to recognize and comment on your skills and abilities, while you downplay, avoid, and doubt your capabilities. Hidden in your heart may be the belief that others are better than you and God blessed you to be an "average" person, at best. Do you avoid new responsibilities because you do not feel you are good enough? Does change overwhelm you? Are you afraid to lead? Do you remain silent and flat when you should speak and then blame it on being shy when honestly you feel ashamed of your educational success or physique? Do you intentionally blend into the walls, hiding your thoughts and yourself because you are embarrassed about your home life, previous life decisions, or sins you have committed? Do you maintain a flat or matte disposition in hopes that others will not be able to observe your imperfections? Is your glossy personality a mask for your insecurities or are you truly vibrant? Your exterior displays are worthy of review.

Accept the New Color

If you answered the questions in the previous sections with an authentic introspection, I am certain that you are aware of the colors your heart displays through your behaviors. These colors may be dark or light or congruent, adjacent, or in direct opposition to God's heart. Notwithstanding the condition, I urge you to accept the fresh coat or alternative hue God wants to use to cover the deficiencies of your heart. This is the area or areas that need to be cleansed or replaced to make you a healthier, improved you. This is the heart God wants to align to His purpose and plan for your life. This is the heart that allows the light of Jesus Christ to shine through to the world. This is the heart that puts you in a place of peace, joy, and contentment. This is the heart that reflects the very purpose for which you were born.

As exciting as it is to upgrade or replace your current heart posture, you must remember that God will not force change; you have to give Him permission to begin His process.

Stay the Course

Just as there are times when painters arrive home with paint and change their minds about the color or determine they do not want to paint; there are occasions when women get to this step and freeze. Because God has disclosed what has to change and hinted at the new heart soon to come; fear is triggered for some. Many decide to postpone or quit the process all together. This is the all-too-familiar, start-and-stop of commitment. You have not totally surrendered to God or His process for cleansing your heart. Perhaps you think you will be missing out on "fun," others in your life will not like the change, or you will no longer fit in with the crowd. Or maybe you are concerned that you will clash with your environment like the papaya orange and hunter green adjacent rooms. Irrespective of your reasoning for the pause, I implore you to at least give God the opportunity to work. Like painting the sample color on your wall, you cannot know the positive impact of the change until you view it in totality.

Accept the color and allow the process to flow until the room is finished, until your color, heart, and life has changed. View God's final masterpiece created in you before you halt the project. To abandon the reconstruction will leave you in worse shape than before with repeated disappointing thoughts of what could have been.

Meditate on the Word of God

Heart Colors

Step 2: Accepting Your Hue

- Am I afraid to know what is in my heart?
- Do my actions reveal an unpleasant heart color?
- Am I afraid others will not accept me?
- Do I trust God for completion of the project?

If you answered yes to any of the questions above, begin the next step of your heart makeover by saying this simple, yet life-changing prayer:

Father,

Thank you for your willingness to cleanse my heart. While I'm not certain of everything in my heart and what it means, I believe that you do. Show me the condition of my heart and reveal what needs to be renewed, redecorated, and rebuilt to align with your will and please you. Show me the color you have chosen for me to complete my destiny and make me beautiful in your sight. Renovate and make me new. I trust you to do it, Lord, in the name of Jesus, amen.

Meditate on the Word of God

Heart Colors

"Search me, God, and know my heart; test me and know my anxious thoughts. See if there is any offensive way in me and lead me in the way everlasting." Psalm 139:23-24

"How many wrongs and sins have I committed? Show me my offense and my sin." Job 13:23

"Remember how the Lord your God led you all the way in the wilderness these forty years, to humble and test you in order to know what was in your heart, whether or not you would keep his commands." Deuteronomy 8:2

Please take a few moments to quiet yourself and listen. The Lord wants to commune with you. ♡

What is the Holy Spirit saying to you? What was highlighted in this chapter? What words resonated with you? What are your instructions? What do you need to do next?

_____
_____
_____
_____
_____
_____
_____
_____

3
Heart Cleanse

Step 3: Discarding the Elephants

Make Room

Before you embark on painting a room, preparation of the space is a necessity; otherwise, you will generate a mid-project disaster with paint displayed in unintended areas. You must relocate all items aligned to the walls such as beds and dressers and place them in the center of the room or eliminate from the room completely. Removing small pieces housed on the surface of large furniture is advised, as this action allows for a more efficient and quick transfer of the big pieces.

If you choose to leave the larger fixtures in the room, it is highly recommended that you cover them with paint cloths or old sheets to protect them from escaping paint. In addition, pictures and electrical outlet covers should be removed, as well as switch covers and draperies. This chore before painting can be daunting, especially if you have a substantial amount of large and small items in the room. Do not fret though, as this system will assist with effective productivity when you do begin to paint.

Because adequate space is required for supplies and the actual painting strokes, this is also the opportune time to remove and discard those unused, broken, and out-of-dated items. Categorizing the objects by significance, utilization, or requirement will aid in the decision to eliminate or retain. It is crucial to resist the temptation to preserve everything, with no respect for the upgraded, efficient room soon to come. After all, fresh paint on the walls of a cluttered room is merely a messy room with new-colored walls. Be forewarned, however, that because you have made the decision to paint and accepted a color, this tedious step can dampen enthusiasm for the finished product. I admonish you, however, to stay the course.

Elephants in the Room

Parallel to prepping a room for painting, your heart renewal requires you to remove, relocate, or eliminate external behaviors and thought processes that God has already identified as detrimental to your complete heart renovation. As a reminder, these actions and mindsets are in direct conflict with the word of God. The oversized behaviors are easily identifiable by you and others in your circle because they are not only incongruent to God's will for His children, but they are also clearly damaging to your overall wellbeing.

Some examples include, but are certainly not limited to, regular occasions of gossiping, cursing, lying, or criticizing others. Do you frequently fornicate, smoke weed, watch pornography, or masturbate? These types of activities definitely serve as large pieces attached to the walls of your heart. You know, without anyone telling you, that in order to please God, you need to stop and adjust these behaviors. These are the elephant-in-the-room activities, that few, including you, confront, although they are recognizable and serve as a reflection of what is inside your heart. Confirmed in the book of Luke, external behaviors identify who you truly are internally. Thus, the type of tree is known by its fruit.

"No good tree bears bad fruit, nor does a bad tree bear good fruit. Each tree is recognized by its own fruit. People do not pick figs from thorn bushes, or grapes from briers."
Luke 6:43-44

An honest acknowledgment of that which you discovered when you accepted your color change will assist you with ridding yourself of all the barriers. Simply remain fixated on the transformed, clean heart God is creating in you, rather than focusing on the prerequisite behavioral changes. These alterations are a part of the process to obtain your new heart. Since you have identified the large items in the rooms of your heart, be determined to remove them.

Top Layers

As you strive to eradicate the sizeable, sin-laced behaviors, you will likely discover that there are other smaller matters housed on top in a multilayered fashion. Like the perfume and jewelry kept on top of the dresser, ofttimes lust, senseless dishonesty, and cigarettes, to name just a few, adorn the surface of fornication, lying, and marijuana. Thus, rumination on your big items will reveal layers of seemingly lesser problems that served as the catalyst for your current state. The quicker you eliminate the smaller matters, the faster the process is to expel the larger ones.

Uncover and Remove

Although superficially easy to paint around without removal, electrical and switch covers should also be displaced before painting. I can assure you from experience, that even the steadiest of hands manage to leave evidence of the old paint or spillage from the new. The same is true in your life. If you resist uncovering matters of the heart and assume you can work around them, your conversion will be partially complete.

In fact, it is guaranteed that with time the hidden issues will resurface and spill over into your renovated life. How many women have hidden childhood molestation accounts that bubble to the top during marriage and lead to struggles with intercourse? Although this issue, like many others, frequently rises in disguise, research into the root cause will reveal that the source is what you kept buried. I implore you to release and allow God to remove every concealed problem so that your makeover will be thorough.

Additionally, merely moving the issues from the forefront to another location and covering them does not remove their impact or allow space for the updated focus God wants to put in you. It isn't just about taking out the old, but it is also about God bringing in the new. What do you have to uncover?

Take this opportunity to examine what is useful in your life and what needs to be discarded from your life and heart. Do you keep behaviors and people near that are useless for your growth? Do they keep you from moving forward and bind you to who you were ten years ago? This is also a time to consider the number of items and people in your life that consistently keep you busy and unfocused from your priorities. Do you have too many Facebook Friends and Instagram Follows that aren't friends at all, but people you feel you need to please with comments, likes, and hours of scrolling?

Space should be generated in your life and your heart to receive what God wants to incorporate. Maintaining your current position probably does not allow time or opportunity for God to occupy. However, your willingness to uncover and eradicate your adverse issues, discard excessive things and people, and make strides to improve allows God the room to truly cleanse your heart and build you anew. Clearing your room and your heart will create space for God to paint the walls with perfection.

Meditate on the Word of God

Heart Cleanse

Step 3: Discarding the Elephants

- Do I have elephants to acknowledge and remove?
- Am I willing to discard the small things that support my elephants?
- Am I willing to relocate or remove things and people that stunt my growth?
- Am I willing to expose everything?
- Do I trust God to complete my heart renovation?

If you answered yes to any of the questions above, begin the next step of your heart makeover by saying this simple, yet life-changing prayer:

Father,

Thank you for your willingness to cleanse me completely. I know there are some obvious elephants in my heart. Help me remove them. Please show me the people and things that keep me bound to who I am. I want to have a clean, pure heart. Thank you, Father, for your grace to endure the painful upheaval of my issues. I believe you will be with me and I trust you to make me new, in the name of Jesus, amen.

Meditate on the Word of God

Heart Cleanse

"Yet if you devote your heart to him and stretch out your hands to him, if you put away the sin that is in your hand and allow no evil to dwell in your tent, then, free of fault, you will lift up your face; you will stand firm and without fear." Job 11:13-15

"What shall we say, then? Shall we go on sinning so that grace may increase? By no means! We are those who have died to sin; how can we live in it any longer?" Romans 6:1-2

"If we confess our sins, he is faithful and just and will forgive us our sins and purify us from all unrighteousness." 1 John 1:9

Please take a few moments to quiet yourself and listen. The Lord wants to commune with you. ♡

What is the Holy Spirit saying to you? What was highlighted in this chapter? What words resonated with you? What are your instructions? What do you need to do next?

_____
_____
_____
_____
_____
_____

4
Heart Attack

Step 4: Taking a Deep Dive

Avoid the Instant Pot

I believe preparing the walls to be painted is the absolute worst step when painting a room. It is tedious, burdensome, and time-consuming. It is the in-the-meantime of life. It is the time when you are waiting on God to move. You're out the wilderness and can see your destiny, but you're not there yet. This phase is most frustrating because at this juncture, the decision to paint has been confirmed, the paint color has been selected and secured, the room has been cleared of large items, and the finished transformation can be visualized.

With eagerness for a completed project, the desire to put color on the walls is immense with heightened momentum to complete the task as quickly as possible. But with all this enthusiasm, you must pause. To receive maximum results, you absolutely cannot leave out this step.

To further clarify the specifics of this stage, prepping a room for paint is like cooking a roast in the Crock-Pot; although the smell offers promise of a wonderful meal, the development is so slow that it deters enthusiasm and often results in an alternative food selection long before the meat is cooked. Because the slow cooker is just that–slow–numerous people have opted to invest in an Instant Pot to get similar results with hastened cooking speeds.

Like purchasing the Instant Pot, many painters evade this preparatory step, pour the paint in the paint tray, begin the strokes, and rush to the finish with compromise of excellence. I caution you to avoid focusing on decreased prep time by cutting corners and avoiding procedures, but rather, use quality products that are suitable for the duties at hand. For example, investing in painter's tape and angled paint brushes as well as soliciting assistance from others for these tedious assignments will speed the process.

I can testify from experience that time will not be gained by omitting painters' tape around windows, baseboards, and crown molding. Inevitably, despite a steady hand and infant-handling-like care, paint almost always manages to coat unintended areas creating a need to double back and scrub paint off undesignated surfaces.

Embrace the Primer

In this room prep stage, dents should also be repaired, and scuff marks removed before you paint a room. Unless the paint shade is very dark, without a paint primer, most abrasions and heavy marks, although initially covered, will invariably stand at attention once the paint dries. These defects will leave your completed work with an unfinished appearance. Therefore, be determined to clean, sand, and prime your walls if you must, to remove intense stains before you paint. Once you review the finished product, you will be thrilled that you spent the extra moments to obtain exceptional results.

Without a doubt, holes must be repaired, which, at times, includes cutting, filling, plastering, sanding, and priming the walls before the paint is applied. Depending on the size of the damage, this fix could take a few minutes to hours to satisfactorily complete. Also, if there are gaps between the interior trim and crown molding, caulk should be used to fill in before painting, otherwise the paint will run, and the clean lines will not exist. Fundamentally, failure to complete these repair measures before painting will result in a room laden with flaws that visibly presents itself as rushed and unfinished.

The Deep Dive

Parallel to the exasperation endured while prepping walls, the most challenging of all the heart renewal segments to withstand is the deep dive. This stage is far beyond acceptance of your large issues, identification of small activities, and acknowledgement of characteristics that block your progress toward a renewed heart. After all, if you are honest, you were already somewhat mindful of many of your strongholds and recognized the need to adjust your behaviors surrounding them. You simply pushed the activities to the background and ignored their negative impact on your life.

This stage is challenging because it is an exhaustive study of the chambers of your heart to identify, cut out, fill, and cover the sources that serve as the *why* behind your choices, decisions, and behaviors. In short, this is God's deep dive into your heart, beyond the surface behaviors to the root causes of your actions. It is God escorting you through your life experiences to reveal the impact and influence of the events on your current and past activities. It is revelation of the DNA-level substance of your heart and comprehension of your triggers that manifest into your distasteful responses. It is managing your core, including idiosyncrasies, values, and beliefs that have been yours for years. Simply, this is God identifying why you behave as you do.

This excursion is almost certain to be uncomfortable, frustrating, and painful; however, I implore you to remain steadfast in seeking revelation because acknowledgement of the foundation of your behaviors is the key component for the healing process and crucial for the new you. If you do not understand the *why*, you are destined to repeat your actions, often with regret and repeated questions like, "Why did I do that again?" and "What was I thinking?"

Potential *Whys*

Although many women's experiences are unique, there are similarities that help explain the *why* behind the performances. Perhaps you have experienced a broken heart, childhood traumas, teenage rebellion, or have made poor adult decisions. Or maybe you have endured events such as drug abuse or parental premature death; these types of occurrences can serve as the *why* behind the manifested behaviors that are contrary to God's word and will for your life.

To further explore, women who are consistently hateful and angry may have been hurt and act from a place of fear. This woman's *why* is not the abrupt, controlling behavior, but rather the angst that resides in her heart. She lives on the defense with the notion that, "I'll get you before you get me" because she secretly believes others intend to hurt her. Moreover, if a woman is extremely passive and disengaged, her *why* could be a result of the guilt she feels from poor decisions made as a young adult or horrific violations against her as a child. Her shame is so elevated that she strives to be unnoticed or even invisible.

You may not be able to identify with the *why's* discussed because there are far too many incidences, statements, and sufferings that serve as the *why* behind the actions of women. Sadly, many of the events have been entombed so far within the heart that there is faint to no knowledge that they exist, even to the woman who carries them. Without the deep dive with God into your heart, there is no way to accurately understand what causes you to behave as you do or to understand the *why* behind your actions.

Foundational Alignment

During this intensely reflective, potentially tumultuous phase, you must also identify your foundational beliefs and ascertain their alignment to God's word. For example, do you fundamentally believe that God exists, and He rewards those that seek Him (Hebrews 11:6b) or that Jesus is the only way to a relationship with God (John 14:6)? Do you deem the Bible to be God's word in print and that these expressions serve as the guide for your life? (2 Timothy 3:16-17)

The Bible is clear that we are to love the Lord our God with all our heart, soul, and mind and our neighbors as ourselves (Matthew 22:37-38) and God's children should think like Jesus Christ, while focusing on things that are true, honest, just, pure, lovely, and of a good report (Philippians 2:5; 4:8). Do these scriptures coincide or clash with your underlying principles and subsequent actions? Do Jesus' teachings align with your thinking and actions? Throughout this segment of your heart restoration, you must sincerely pinpoint that which resides in your heart that is united to God's will and eliminate the rest. This process is identifying the dents, scrapes, and holes in your heart that were created by and remain from life's journey. This is the scraping the corners of your heart and submission to God in preparation for His paint and redecoration of your heart and life.

A Snail's Pace

This phase of the heart change, like prepping the room, is typically gradual because acknowledgement of the core issues and change of your thinking patterns take focused time to accept and alter. Paul teaches us about transforming the mind in the book of Romans, *"And be not conformed to this world: but be ye transformed by the renewing of your mind, that ye may prove what is that good, and acceptable, and perfect, will of God."* (Romans 12:2)

Given permission, however, God will usher you through your life and reveal the source of your behaviors. Like prepping the room for a fresh coat of paint, God will repair your holes and dents and gently cover your wounds with His primer of love and healing before making you anew. His primer, like that used in a room, will ensure your new heart is sealed without fear of your old life bleeding through.

While it may seem as though God is hurting or even trying to kill you as He forces you to relive unpleasant and traumatic moments, rest assured that He is repairing your imperfections. God visualizes the finished room: your polished heart. He knows that neglecting this portion of your cleansing will ultimately leave you unfinished and incomplete. He loves you too much to rush the process, but rather He will take the time to refurbish your heart without compromise. Trust God, as He sees your clean heart and knows your destiny's end.

Meditate on the Word of God

Heart Attack

Step 4: Taking a Deep Dive

- Am I afraid to know the why?
- Am I able to withstand the pain?
- Am I willing to uncover that which I have hidden?
- Do I trust God to complete my heart renovation?

If you answered yes to any of the questions above, begin the next step of your heart makeover by saying this simple, yet life-changing prayer:

Father,

Thank you for loving me enough to completely heal me. I am afraid to discover my whys, but I know that you are with me and you're doing what is best for me to be whole. Thank you for staying close to me during this hard time and preparing my heart to be brand new. I trust you to finish that which you have started in me. I trust you to renovate my heart. Thank you for revealing and healing the whys behind my behaviors, in the name of Jesus, amen.

Meditate on the Word of God

Heart Attack

"Your beauty should not come from outward adornment, such as elaborate hairstyles and the wearing of gold jewelry or fine clothes. Rather, it should be that of your inner self, the unfading beauty of a gentle and quiet spirit, which is of great worth in God's sight." 1 Peter 3:3-4

"Search me, God, and know my heart; test me and know my anxious thoughts. See if there is any offensive way in me, and lead me in the way everlasting." Psalm 139:23-24

"I will praise you with an upright heart as I learn your righteous laws." Psalm 119:7

Please take a few moments to quiet yourself and listen. The Lord wants to commune with you. ♡

What is the Holy Spirit saying to you? What was highlighted in this chapter? What words resonated with you? What are your instructions? What do you need to do next?

_____
_____
_____
_____
_____
_____
_____

5
Heart Stent

Step 5: Receiving the Strokes

Paint Your Walls

Now that you have decided to paint; the color has been selected; large and small items have been removed or covered; switch plates have been separated; holes, dents, and scrapes have been repaired; walls have been primed; woodwork has been taped; and the corners have been cleaned, you are *finally* ready to put color on your walls! Not surprisingly, this step, like all the others, requires a specific order and methods to produce a complete, professional-like finish.

Ventilation

Before you open the paint, it is important to raise a window and utilize a fan to provide ventilation from the paint fumes. Depending on the type of paint, oil-based or latex, and the level of volatile organic compounds contained in them, gases from the mixture are released into the atmosphere. These fumes can irritate your eyes, nose, or throat or cause headaches, dizziness, or nausea, especially when you fail to provide adequate air circulation. To complete your project with stamina and confidence and without illness, do not omit this simple step.

Follow the Steps

Once you have properly ventilated the room, stir the paint with a paint stick and pour into the paint tray. To obtain the best results, resist the urge to dip your roller and begin stroking the walls. Instead, grab a two-inch wide brush and paint the walls along the ceiling, floors, and woodwork with smooth strokes, holding the brush as you would a pencil. Following this method will decrease errors with paint splatters in unintended areas and provide more freedom with the paint roller in the near future.

To fill in the wall color, work in small sections starting from the top of the wall and slowly moving the roller in a zig-zag pattern with overlapping lines until you have covered the entire walls. Using this systematic approach will ensure comprehensive and even coverage of the paint. Upon completion, lightly roll over the painted areas a second time from the ceiling downward. This step will remove paint runs and buildup and generate an even distribution of the paint.

The final action for painting a room is covering the wall trim. This step should only be started once the walls are completely dry. Failure to exercise patience during the dry-time will wreck this crucial preparation and probably ruin your expert-like finish with mixed paint colors.

Once the walls are fully dried, apply painter's tape along the wall trim edges and secure with a plastic putty knife or other utensil that will flatten the tape. (Unconventionally, I have used a plastic kitchen spatula to successfully accomplish this task.) Once you finish painting the trim with a small brush, slowly and carefully remove the painter's tape. Do not wait for the paint to dry. If the paint fully dries on the trim, it is apt to peel and create the need for repeat coverage.

Mold

Similar to the actual room painting phase, you are now ready receive the transformational covering of the Lord. You made the choice and gave God permission to change your heart; acknowledged and sought God's assistance with removal of your blatant and small sin-laced behaviors; withstood the upheaval, frustration, and pain of your deep issues; accepted the why behind your behaviors; and allowed God to readjust and align your thinking patterns and succeeding actions to His will. Without completion of these phases, your heart facelift would have been like painting walls that were fortified with mold. While the paint would have provided momentary coverage and a beautiful appearance, eventually the fungus would have resurfaced and destroyed the laborious efforts dedicated to the makeover.

If God would have simply given you a glow and temporary peace without requiring an authentic heart cleansing, you would return to your familiar and dull ways within months or even days. (Have you experienced this before? You thought you were cleansed and ready for your destiny, only to find yourself stuck on stupid, again?) Ecstatically, because you braved God's cleansing process, He will now begin to seal your heart and cover you with His presence, peace, and glory!

Trust His Covering

Much like the necessary ventilation when painting a room, it will benefit you to obtain a confidant with whom you can discuss your process and progress, including frustrations, pain, and victories, as it is probable at this stage that you are quite weary. (Please note: I said *a* confidant, not a few or many. Not everyone needs or even cares to know the intimate details of your heart.)

Your exposed situations may have been so egregious that

you remain somewhat apprehensive and unsteady with concerns that the issues will return or never be completely covered. Just remember that there are times when we all become weak and need encouragement to complete the tasks before us, especially when the journey has been long and difficult. The Bible teaches us, however, that we will receive a reward if we stay the course and finish the race.

> *"Let us not become weary in doing good, for at the proper time we will reap a harvest if we do not give up."*
> **Galatians 6:9**

This is the time that you must trust God's methods and the power of His covering strokes. After all, you can be certain that God's grace is sufficient, and His strength is made perfect in our weakness. (2 Corinthians 12:9)

Top-Down Approach

God's revelation and washing of the heart also corresponds to the proper top-down paint stoke methods described. Throughout this development, He began to highlight the noticeable external behaviors housed on surface of your heart. From these large, unaligned actions to the deep, hidden matters, God primarily worked downward to the heart's core with slow and delicate disclosures. If God revealed everything that needed to be cleaned, adjusted, or removed at once, you would have had the propensity to become overwhelmed and never allowed Him to start the process or eloped long before He finished the overhaul.

Instead, God worked in small sections of your cleansing matters with a zig-zag and overlapping approach to expose areas in contrast to His will. He gradually showed you how your behaviors and issues interconnected and influenced one another. Hence, He may have disclosed that you have a habit of criticizing that is due to your low self-esteem formed from your childhood isolation and nurtured through adult rejection. Regardless of the interweave and connections, you can be certain that He has sealed and covered everything without leaving any area opened or unfinished.

Changed, Let it Go!

At this stage, you have likely transformed so much that your excitement for the finished product, your renovated self, may convince you to move forward ahead of God's timing and display yourself to the world. I advise you to exert caution and wait on God to complete the final step, as moving ahead of Him will probably cause a setback. You do not have to be concerned that He will not finish your heart project.

What may seem like a delay or desertion to you is God's perfect orchestration and precise timing. You can trust Him to complete the project you granted Him permission to begin. It is vital to remember that God keeps His word.

"God is not human, that he should lie, not a human being, that he should change his mind. Does he speak and then not act? Does he promise and not fulfil?" Numbers 23:19

Equally important is that you cast aside fear and move when God commands. If you remain fixated on your past mistakes, you are not permitting God to cover your heart, although He has already forgiven you. Keep in mind that God does not force Himself on anyone; you have to be willing to accept the clean-hearted you. Now that He has cleansed your heart, your way of thinking and actions should follow suit. Some of the behaviors that you once considered exciting or fun should not hold the same value and in fact, may be appalling to you now. This is the *you-know-a-tree-by-its-fruit* concept—what is in the heart is manifested in behaviors.

In the apostle Paul's letter to the Romans, he reminds the believers that Jesus covered their sin with His blood shed on Calvary.

> *"Therefore, there is now no condemnation for those who are in Christ Jesus." Romans 8:1*

You do not need to hold on to that which God released! If you follow God's timing and move as He instructs, you will be able to stand with assurance that you have been washed and your heart is presentable with His perfect covering. Philippians 1:6 assures us that God will accomplish that which He starts.

> *And I am certain that God, who began the good work within you, will continue his work until it is finally finished on the day when Christ Jesus returns."*
> *Philippians. 1:6 NLT*

Believe God and His word. Trust His change and let the rest go.

Meditate on the Word of God

Heart Stent

Step 5: Receiving the Strokes

- Do I believe God has changed my heart?
- Am I afraid my old mess will resurface?
- Am I afraid I'm not completely covered?
- Do I trust God to complete my heart renovation?

If you answered yes to any of the questions above, begin the next step of your heart makeover by saying this simple, yet life-changing prayer:

Father,

Thank you for cleansing my heart and covering it so the old behaviors and thoughts don't take over. I believe your word is true and that you do not lie. Thank you for painting my heart. Thank you for making me new, thank you for loving me enough to complete the project in me, in the name of Jesus, amen.

Meditate on the Word of God

Heart Stent

"If we confess our sins, He is faithful and just and will forgive us our sins and purify us from all unrighteousness." 1 John 1:9

"Trust in the L<small>ORD</small> with all your heart and lean not on your own understanding; in all your ways submit to him, and he will make your paths straight." Proverbs 3:5-6

"'For I know the plans I have for you, declares the L<small>ORD</small>, 'plans to prosper you and not to harm you, plans to give you hope and a future.'" Jeremiah 29:11

Please take a few moments to quiet yourself and listen. The Lord wants to commune with you. ♡

What is the Holy Spirit saying to you? What was highlighted in this chapter? What words resonated with you? What are your instructions? What do you need to do next?

_____

_____

_____

_____

_____

_____

_____

6
Heart Recovery
Step 6: Coming Together Again

What Must Go?

Now that your paint project is complete, you will need to reassemble the room with items essential for functionality, comfort, and beautification. Refrain from reintroducing furniture and objects that were determined in the destruction phase to be no longer useful or relevant for the new, updated space. Clutter in the room distracts from the fresh color uplift.

It is also important to note that with every painted room, there is typically a change in the look and feel of the furniture you opted to retain. With this new view, you are now forced to decide if the furniture should remain in the new space as it is, be updated, or be replaced with more satisfactory items. Sometimes no matter what you do, the pieces are no longer suitable, and you simply have to replace them and start anew. Selecting the complimentary furniture color scheme and atmosphere desired in advance will assist you with determining the appropriate decorative pieces for the room.

Where Does It Fit?

Once you have decided on the objects to complete your room,

placement becomes a priority. I would encourage you to consider not only functionality of the objects, but also space for maneuvering throughout the room and into others. A correct flow in the room helps produce a pleasant environment with desired occupancy and movement into adjoining rooms. To help you decide, you may also want to solicit insight from a trusted friend who is intimately acquainted with your personality and style. Reassembling your room should be exciting and the completion should offer a refreshing, positive space for you to enjoy.

The Volcano

How do you reassemble your life after your heart, thinking, and behavior have been changed? How do you decide what and who no longer adds value to your life? While you may be ecstatic about the refurbishment, be forewarned that everyone in your circle may not be happy about your transformation. In fact, they may candidly oppose your changes and tell you, "You've changed," "You think you're better than us," or "You're not fun anymore," "You're crazy and brainwashed."

Although these statements may be hurtful, they may not all be false because your heart change changed you. You will talk and behave noticeably different than before and even if you try to retain your old routines, it will feel strange. When God alters your heart, the core of your existence, everything else about you aligns to it. Imagine watching a volcano erupt. Although you see gases, ash, rocks, and lava expelled from the mouth of the mountain, everything is formed from the disruption deep in the earth's crust.

In other words, what you see in the atmosphere and on the ground comes from one source. Equally, what you now experience and what other witness stems from your heart change. When God modifies and improves your heart, you are more like Him and less like the world. You have changed and most people, unfortunately, prefer the antecedent.

Moving On

Given the reality of your updated persona, you must decide what and who is appropriate for your improved space. Reflect on what and who benefits your life. Who complements you and challenges you to grow? Consider the usefulness and comfort, as well as the distractions and strongholds that each item and person add to your life. Be determined to discard the behaviors and people that represent who you used to be. Those things and people that supported and fed your negative behaviors and dispositions must be eliminated or you will find yourself inching back to your old life. It doesn't mean that the individuals or things are worthless or even bad, but it does communicate that their place in your life is no longer healthy or necessary.

Some people will decide for you, as they are attached to their current state and determined not to move for anyone. They remain steadfast in their present situation with resilience and change is not an option. Without your assistance, these acquaintances will distance themselves from you, as your change is a constant reminder of their own stagnant position and this sometimes makes them resentful.

With fewer friendships and a more organized heart, God will begin to send new people with kindred priorities into your environment. These people will understand your process, progress, and upgrade with acceptance of who you are: the reassembled you.

Meditate on the Word of God
Heart Recovery

Step 6: Coming Together Again

- Am I afraid of losing friends?
- Am I uncomfortable deciding who stays?
- Am I afraid of my new world?
- Do I trust God to complete my heart renovation?

If you answered yes to any of the questions above, begin the next step of your heart makeover by saying this simple, yet life-changing prayer:

Father,

I trust you. I wish everyone could accept my changes and stay in my life, but I understand why they must go. I want you more than them. Help me to know what stays and what should go, including friends and even family. Thank you in advance for bringing new, like-minded people into my life. I love and thank you for my heart renovation, in the name of Jesus, amen.

Meditate on the Word of God
Heart Recovery

"For God is not a God of disorder but of peace—as in all the congregations of the Lord's people."
1 Corinthians 14:33

*"The L*ORD* makes firm the steps of the one who delights in him; though he may stumble, he will not fall, for the Lord upholds him with his hand."*
Psalm 37:23-24

"Order my steps in your word; let no sin rule over me."
Psalm 119:133

Please take a few moments to quiet yourself and listen. The Lord wants to commune with you. ♡

What is the Holy Spirit saying to you? What was highlighted in this chapter? What words resonated with you? What are your instructions? What do you need to do next?

_____
_____
_____
_____
_____
_____

7
Heart Maintenance
Step 7: Retaining Your Health

Preservation

You've prepared, prepped, painted, and pampered your room until it became the environment you desired: suited and ready for use. Now, how do you preserve your refreshed, occupied room? Light maintenance and intentional care can extend the life of the paint and beauty of your surroundings.

To being with, accept that the initial spotless room is only for a season because with use, the walls will eventually need to be spot cleaned and touched up and, after an extended time, painted with fresh strokes. After a few weeks of settling into the room, use a soft cloth with a very mild soap solution to gently wipe the walls and remove dust and dirt. If you have already acquired stains and marks, you will need to use more penetrating force to remove them.

Additionally, if nicks and dents are present, the stored leftover paint should be used to touch up the deficiencies and match the paint color. If the dents are deep, applying feather-like strokes around the area will blend the paint color and mask the flaw. These simple methods will preserve the appearance in your room.

Daily Cleanse

Unlike the spot check and gentle care for your walls, maintaining a clean heart requires steady examination, submission, repentance, and obedience. This consistent cleansing is needed because we dwell in the sin-infested earth with temptations always around us. To help keep your heart from attracting the attitudes, behaviors, and dispositions of the world, obedience is key. Hence, it is necessary to study the Bible and pray each day with intentional focus, honest heart checks, and surrender to God for His cleansing and will to be done in your life. In particular, if you follow Jesus' example, you will seek an audience with God before sunrise.

"Very early in the morning, while it was still dark, Jesus got up, left the house and went off to a solitary place, where he prayed." Mark 1:35

I absolutely cannot overemphasize the importance of pursuing an audience with God daily. Being in His presence regularly builds your relationship, moves you into a more intimate fellowship and ultimately keeps your heart molded to His. The word of God teaches us in 2 Corinthians that the more focused time we spend with God, the more we begin to understand His ways and develop into His likeness.

"And we all, who with unveiled faces contemplate the Lord's glory, are being transformed into his image with ever-increasing glory, which comes from the Lord, who is the Spirit." 2 Corinthians 3:18

Hence, the more personal time you spend with God the more you become like Him. Please highlight, understand, and know that this time is not exclusive to the church, as being inside the building does not equate to or guarantee a connection. It is the personal bond between you and God that keeps your heart clean.

Relationship Development

While your connection with God is distinctive from any other relationship you have had or will ever have, there are some fundamental principles that can assist you with understanding the developmental process. In the initial stages of almost all relationships, the couple spends substantial amounts of time daily talking and texting. They typically discuss a multitude of topics and gather information about each other including characteristics, values, beliefs, expectations, and the like. They are simply getting to know one another past the surface observations to the essence of the person. There is also a strong desire to spend quality time in each other's presence to not only observe body language, but also to simply share space.

It is exciting to be together physically and emotionally. With prolonged quality time, you learn the other person so well that you can predict his responses to your questions, calculate his actions in particular situations, and foresee his opinions regarding various issues. In fact, because you have spent so much time with him, you not only know his acts, but you understand his ways and are able to finish his sentences. You are usually so connected at this point that your thinking patterns and mannerism are linked.

Developing your relationship with God is no different. He longs to spend time with you listening and talking. He wants you to desire to know Him, how He thinks, what He does, and how He operates. He wants to show you how important you are to Him and that He loves you. In fact, the more time you spend with Him in sincere prayer and reading His word, the more you become intimate with Him and take on His characteristics, including transformation of your heart to mimic His. Moses developed this closeness with God because he spent time with Him; not only talking but listening.

> *"Moses was there with the LORD forty days and forty nights without eating bread or drinking water. And he wrote on the tablets the words of the covenant—the Ten Commandments." Exodus 34:28*

Your intimacy can be so close that you, like Moses, can become familiar with God's ways and not just His actions. "*He made known His ways unto Moses, His acts unto the children of Israel.*" (Psalm 103:7) In essence, remaining intimately connected to God keeps your heart postured for purification.

Also akin to Moses, when the man after God's own heart (1 Samuel 13:14; Acts 13:22), King David, committed adultery with Bathsheba, he penned words begging God to clean his heart, demonstrating the need for consistent cleansing.

> *"Create in me a pure heart, O God, and renew a steadfast spirit within me." Psalm 51:10*

Like us, King David was not a morally pure man, but he was committed to God and knew that his transgressions, whether big or small, were against God. Because King David knew this, he quickly approached God with a repentant heart and asked for forgiveness with each incident. (Psalm 32; Psalm 51; 2 Samuel 12)

Vitally, just as it requires intentional care to maintain your painted room, it takes incessant cycling of surrender, acceptance of the deficiencies, discard of the defects and trust the Master Painter's covering to keep your heart pure before God. Following the steps to paint your room and heart will preserve your heart's harmonious connection to God's heart and His will for your life.

Meditate on the Word of God

Heart Maintenance

Step 7: Retaining Your Health

- Am I scared of the heart maintenance?
- Am I worried my heart will become flawed again?
- Am I concerned about communicating with God?
- Do I trust God to communicate with me?

If you answered yes to any of the questions above, maintain your heart makeover by saying this simple, yet life-changing prayer:

Father,

Thank you for cleaning my heart and making me presentable to you. Father, I know I can't keep my heart clean on my own, but I believe you can. I want to communicate with you, but sometimes I don't know how. Please help me to hear your voice and know when you're speaking without words. I trust you to keep my heart clean as I stay in your presence. Thank you for allowing me to have a relationship with you and help me to assist others with this process, in the name of Jesus, amen.

Meditate on the Word of God

Heart Maintenance

"How can a young man keep his way pure? By guarding it according to your word." Psalm 119:9

"So, flee youthful passions and pursue righteousness, faith, love and peace, along with those who call on the Lord from a pure heart." 2 Timothy 2:22

"For sin shall no longer be your master, because you are not under the law, but under grace." Romans 6:14

Please take a few moments to quiet yourself and listen. The Lord wants to commune with you. ♡

What is the Holy Spirit saying to you? What was highlighted in this chapter? What words resonated with you? What are your instructions? What do you need to do next?

_____

_____

_____

_____

_____

_____

_____

_____

_____

_____

8
Summary

Oh Lord…Paint My Room was not written to deliver a step-by-step method to paint a room. But rather, this book was penned to provide you with the systematic approach God uses to cleanse the hearts of His children. Because God's strategic methods are parallel to the procedures used to paint a room, this book offers a bonus: two books in one. Not only does it outline instructions for properly painting a room, it more importantly ushers you through the measures to obtain and retain a redecorated heart from God. If you are interested in studying the correct paint steps, simply review the chapters. The focus of this summary will be to highlight and review the heart renewal process.

There are seven simple, yet intricate, steps to adhere to if you desire a renewed heart from God. Because God uses a methodical approach to cleanse the hearts of His children, it is not optional to omit any part of the process. Likened to painting a room and obtaining professional results, God's heart makeover is complete only when all procedures are followed. Cutting corners or skipping steps will lead to extended time and additional work, not to mention the obvious flawed results. Thus, receiving a refurbished heart requires following specific directions and usually more time than the receiver anticipates. With this in mind, I encourage you to remain focused and develop an unwavering commitment to your target outcome: a clean heart. The reward is absolutely worth the cost of the process.

Initially, you must decide that you need God to clean your heart. This decision cannot be a half-hearted desire based solely on Sunday morning high praise or the desire to impress someone. Rather, this choice should be from a rock-bottom state, a sick-and-tired-of-being-sick-and-tired place coupled with a craving to know and please God while in His presence. Making the decision to have your heart dressed means not only surrendering, but also giving God permission to take you through His method to shape you as He desires. I can assure you that at the completion of the process, there will be no regrets and you will be overjoyed and amazed by the results.

Once you have committed to the cleanse, you must acknowledge the state of your heart and accept God's revelation of what needs to be changed. This is God selecting a new paint color for you. As He shows you what is in your heart that is contrary to His will and character, you will need to begin to remove these items, or in other words, prepare your heart for His makeover. These thought processes and behavior patterns are typically a part of your everyday actions and have become what you have likely deemed "just the way I am."

Upon ejection of these top-level behaviors, God will begin to take you on a deep dive into your heart. While this step is often painful, it is crucial for you to discover the *why* behind your actions and ultimately to be able to destroy the roots of your beliefs and actions that are not aligned with God. Because this phase of the process is laden with revelation, it is highly suggested that you increase your time of reflection, prayer, and reading of God's word.

With preparation of your heart complete, you are now ready to receive God's color covering to seal and beautify the renovated

Summary

you. You can be certain that His strokes will be delicate, complete, and perfect. In fact, God's change is so astounding, that others will notice a change in you. Some will embrace your transformation, while others will refuse to accept your upgrade. In the face of this rejection, it is important that you remember some people, like the furniture in the newly painted room, will no longer compliment your environment. You must sustain your focus on God and target goal for keeping a clean heart before Him.

You will preserve your refreshed heart with continuous surrender, prayer, and obedience. This heart maintenance and your determination will deepen your relationship with God and take you from glory to glory in His presence. Complete trust in the *Paint Master* is required.

Meditate on the Word of God

Summary

- What was my most difficult stage?
- How do I feel about the renewed me?
- What is my maintenance plan?
- How will I share my process with others to help them?

Answering the questions above will help you review your process and maintain a clean heart before God.

Father,

Thank you for purifying my heart. Keep your hand on me and keep me from evil. Raise your spirit in me and make me more like you, in the name of Jesus, amen.

Summary

Meditate on the Word of God
Summary

"Therefore, if anyone is in Christ, the new creation has come: The old has gone, the new is here!"
2 Corinthians 5:17

"I delight in your decrees; I will not neglect your word."
Psalm 119:16

"My heart, O God, is steadfast, my heart is steadfast; I will sing and make music." Psalm 57:7

Please take a few moments to quiet yourself and listen. The Lord wants to commune with you. ♡

What is the Holy Spirit saying to you? What was highlighted in this chapter? What words resonated with you? What are your instructions? What do you need to do next?

_____
_____
_____
_____
_____
_____
_____
_____
_____
_____

P.O. Box 453
Powder Springs, Georgia 30127
770.727.6517

info@entegritypublishing.com
www.entegritypublishing.com

CPSIA information can be obtained
at www.ICGtesting.com
Printed in the USA
JSHW020003200323
39126JS00005B/19